Deborah Nourse Lattimore

PUNGA
THE GODDESS OF UGLY

Harcourt Brace & Company

SAN DIEGO   NEW YORK   LONDON

PUNGA

THE GODDESS OF UGLY

Deborah Nourse Lattimore

Library of Congress Cataloging-in-Publication Data
Lattimore, Deborah Nourse.
Punga, goddess of ugly/Deborah Nourse Lattimore. — 1st ed.
p.   cm.
Summary: Because of their bravery and understanding of Maori traditions when they outwit Punga, the goddess of ugly, a pair of twin sisters earn the highly revered chin tattoo called a moko.
ISBN 0-15-292862-6
I. Maori (New Zealand people) — Juvenile fiction. [1. Maori (New Zealand people) — Fiction. 2. Twins — Fiction. 3. Sisters — Fiction. 4. New Zealand — Fiction.] I. Title.
PZ7.L36998Pu   1993
[E] — dc20   92-23191

First edition
A B C D E

Printed in Singapore

The illustrations in this book were done in Winsor & Newton tube watercolors and overlayed with Berol Prismacolor and Lyre pencils on D'Arches hot-press watercolor paper.
The display type for the title was hand-painted by the illustrator, based on Informal 1001 BT.
The text type was set in Cloister by Thompson Type, San Diego, California.
Color separations by Bright Arts, Ltd., Singapore
Production supervision by Warren Wallerstein and David Hough
Designed by Lori J. McThomas

To Diane D'Andrade

and appreciation to Betty Nicholas and the
Department of Defense Dependents Schools

Once not very long ago there were twin sisters, Kiri and Maraweia.
They lived on the North Island with their grandmother, who taught them
all about Maori ways. She hoped the girls would earn a fine *moko*, a chin
tattoo, to show they had learned well and had come of age.

One summer's night, Grandmother, Kiri, and Maraweia sat beside the

fire and gazed upward as the clouds billowed and climbed.

"Did we weave the *tukutuku* cloth well today, Grandmother?" asked Kiri.

"Yes," replied Grandmother. "And you know almost all the songs and stories of our people, too. But you need to practice the *haka* dance. It is not yet right."

"Look," said Kiri. "There, in the clouds! It looks like Mudfish and Lizard dancing the *haka!*" She stood up, raised her arms, and began to dance.

Maraweia, too, stood up, but as she swayed, she went from serious to silly in no time at all. She stuck out her tongue and gurgled at her sister.

"Maraweia," said Grandmother, "the *haka* dance should be beautiful. When you stick out your tongue, be fierce and full of power, have *mana*, or you will seem ugly. You will look more like Mudfish and Lizard than a beautiful Maori girl. And you know what happened to them, don't you?" Grandmother paused. "Yes," she said, "you know."

Grandmother's eyes sparkled in the fire's glow and strands of her hair shone like quicksilver. She patted the mat beside her and the girls sat down.

"You remember, there was a time — oh, so long ago — when all the creatures went their ways in the world. All that walked or crawled or flew went with Tane, god of the earth. All that swam went with Tangeroa, god of the sea. But Mudfish and Lizard frolicked in and out of the waves at the edge of the sea, and they were left behind. 'You caused us to be left out!' shouted Lizard. 'Blame yourself, scaly one!' said Mudfish. And they danced faster and faster and finally stuck out their tongues as far as they would go and wiggled their tongues in a very ugly way.

"Suddenly Punga, the goddess of everything ugly, appeared. Seeing that her brothers had divided up all the animals between them, she growled and stamped her feet and stuck out her tongue, too. Mudfish and Lizard made one last ugly face and — POOF! — all three vanished."

"Where did they go?" asked Kiri.

"Deep into the heart of this island," said Grandmother, "to the lodge house of Punga. It is hidden by a circle of great, dark trees, and no one knows exactly where it is. But it is said that Lizard and Mudfish are stuck there on the lodgepole, like wood, to teach them a lesson for making themselves ugly."

Kiri and Maraweia sat staring into the flickering, sputtering flames and smoke, where strange, grinning faces seemed to rise and fall.

"Will they ever be free?" asked Kiri.

"Well, Punga does let them dance once a year, when a breeze rustles the trees and the moon is full — as it is tonight," Grandmother said. Her voice trailed off and she lay down to sleep.

Kiri and Maraweia lay down, too, but their eyes filled with the shapes of clouds dancing across the face of the moon.

"Maraweia," said Kiri. "I am glad we are not stuck up on Punga's lodge

house, aren't you? We'd never earn a fine *moko* like Grandmother's."

"Or maybe we will get *mokos* that look like this!" laughed Maraweia, wiggling her tongue around and giggling.

"Maraweia, why do you always make such ugly faces?" Kiri asked.

But Maraweia paid no attention to Kiri. She wiggled her tongue around and flopped her arms like a mudfish, then crawled through the air like a lizard and raced off through the trees.

Kiri chased after her. They went skipping over black supplejack vines and *kawakawa* plants, heavy and shuddering with night dew. The sky grew darker and darker. On and on they went until at last Kiri and Maraweia found themselves in a clearing encircled by ancient *kahikatea* trees. A shiver raced up Kiri's spine. Through the rising patches of lowland fog she saw the shapes of snarling teeth; long, twisting tongues; and a single pair of *paua* shell eyes glowering down at them. And still, Maraweia

gurgled and giggled and twiddled her tongue this way and that.

"Stop, Maraweia! Stop!" Kiri gasped. But it was too late. "POOF!"

Maraweia was gone! Kiri flew around the walls of the great lodge house like a frightened fantail. A low, hideous laugh rushed down from the roof like a waterfall. There, just beneath the roof pole, was Punga, the goddess of ugly. And at her feet was Maraweia, as stiff as wood, with her tongue stuck all the way out!

"Aaaah!" cried Kiri. She scrambled from the clearing, plunging into the tangled woods. She thought of Grandmother asleep on her mat, her eyes closed, peaceful in the quiet of the night. What could Kiri say to her? She must get her sister back, or they would never earn their *mokos*. She felt her sister call her. She knew she had to go back. So Kiri, though her heart was leaping, danced the fiercest, strongest *haka* she could and turned around.

When Kiri arrived at the clearing, the clouds broke apart and the moon shone down like rivulets of silver. Fragrant night breezes swept down from the towering trees and their leaves rustled in whispering rhythms. Kiri held her breath. She watched in amazement as Lizard and Mudfish came down from Punga's lodge house and slowly began to step and sway. In the moonlight Lizard's scales shone like diamonds and Mudfish's fins shimmered like silk gossamer. Together they danced the *haka* just as Kiri had tried to do.

"How beautiful!" Kiri exclaimed in surprise.

"Did you say I was beautiful?" asked Lizard, holding up his tail.

"I thought you said *I* was beautiful," replied Mudfish, and she spread out her fins in the air.

"When you dance the *haka* like that, you *are* beautiful," said Kiri. "And it is the way I want to dance, too."

"Beautiful?" thundered a voice from the roof of the lodge house.

Kiri stood up straight. She raised her arms. She was ready for Punga.

"Yes! To dance the *haka* is a beautiful thing, a fierce Maori thing," she replied. "Give me my sister to dance with, and I will show you. If you are really the goddess of everything ugly, you should have only ugly things on your lodge house. Let us all dance the *haka* together and if any one of us is ugly, that one should be on your roof beam for all to see!"

Punga smiled, her curled teeth showing beneath her tongue. She emerged from the murmuring darkness and brought a trembling Maraweia with her.

"Show me this dance, then," said Punga, and her eyes glinted in the moonlight.

And so they danced. Lizard twisted and crawled and stuck out his tongue with great beauty and strength. He was not ugly.

"Be gone!" shouted Punga. "You belong to Tane, not me!"

Mudfish filled her fins with night breeze and turned gracefully around and delicately stuck out her tongue. And she was not ugly.

"Be gone!" shouted Punga. "You belong with Tangeroa, not me!"

Then Kiri and Maraweia danced. For once Maraweia followed her sister carefully, bending her trembling knees, clasping her hands exactly and standing straight. Kiri and Maraweia proudly lifted their chins, faced Punga, and slowly stuck out their tongues. All of a sudden Kiri and Maraweia felt beautiful, fierce, and happy. They had danced the *haka* together perfectly. And as they stood together in the clearing, the breezes stilled, and they felt calm inside.

"What is that on your chins?" snapped Punga, pointing.

"Kiri!" exclaimed Maraweia. "You have a *moko!*"

"If I do, surely it is magic," said Kiri. "And you have one, too!
A beautiful one!"

"A *moko?*" grunted Punga. "It looks like this to me!" And she stuck out her tongue and growled and wiggled it around this way and that.

"Ooooh, *that* is ugly!" said the twins.

POOF! Punga vanished with a terrible howl.

Kiri and Maraweia bolted from the clearing and did not look behind them until they stood at the porch of their own house. Grandmother was waiting for them.

"Oh!" said Grandmother. "You are back! I awoke and you were both gone." Then she looked closer. "Your chins! What magic is this?"

"We found Punga's lodge house, Grandmother," said Kiri, "and we danced with Lizard and Mudfish and . . ."

"And we stuck out our tongues at Punga, too," added Maraweia.

"Ah, then," said Grandmother smiling, "you finally learned not to wiggle your tongue the wrong way."

"Yes, Grandmother," they replied, and looking at each other said, "but we know someone who hasn't learned yet!"

Author's Note

How far can *you* stick out your tongue? Could you stick out your tongue, lift your arms to the sky, and dance backward gracefully? Without getting silly? It's not as easy as you might think.

The country we know as New Zealand, which is also called Aotearoa, is composed of two islands located in Eastern Polynesia near Australia. The ancestors of the native people, the Maori, arrived in New Zealand from Western Polynesia around A.D. 800, and today they still raise sheep, produce wool, and carve beautiful lodge house sculptures. The Maori do a dance called the *haka*, which is performed with the dancers' tongues sticking out, and which they consider beautiful, fierce, and exciting. Imagine winning battles by sticking out your tongue! The Maori do it. Warriors stand in two lines facing each other and stick out their tongues. The side that keeps its tongue out for the longest time wins.

Now that you've read about Punga, the goddess of all things ugly, you may want to learn more about the Maori. If you do, you may discover that the morepork, a kind of owl, is your ancestor spirit watching over you with big, bright eyes, and that there are secret meanings to some special trees and flowers. The less said about something, the more mysterious! I have hidden pictures with special meanings in the illustrations in this book. If you want to know their secrets, look carefully. The glossary will help. And remember, sometimes, just sometimes, in the right time and place, sticking out your tongue can be a fierce and beautiful and *difficult* thing to do — especially if the right person is watching!

Glossary

Clematis   Beautiful white blossoms that can mean either sadness or celebration.

Fantail   A restless, nervous bird, considered a bad omen.

Flax   A fibrous plant good for making *tukutuku* cloth.

Gecko   The green lizard brought to New Zealand by the ancestor Wheketoro as a pet, considered *tapu*.

Golden Tainui   A yellow flowering plant used as a medicine to ward off bad spirits.

Hinau   A palmlike plant whose fruits are considered delicious but that is difficult to climb, hence the saying "A man who climbs the hinau tree is food for the roots!"

Huia   An orange-cheeked bird whose white-tipped feathers are worn by people of rank.

Kahikatea   Very tall trees that are said to have sprouted from feathers of a bird who carried the ancestor Pourangahua to New Zealand.

Kakariki   Parakeets, known for their constant gossiping.

Kawakawa   A plant associated with death.

Kidney fern   A fern shaped like a kidney, worn in sadness.

Kokako   A trickster bird who masquerades as a Huia.

Koromiko   A plant that means stay-at-home because it often grows next to the lodge house.

Lizard   Also called *Tuatara*, a *tapu* animal brought to New Zealand by mythic ancestors.

Moko   A face tattoo. Just the chin is tattooed on women, the whole face on men.

Morepork   An owl, a guardian ancestor spirit, who appears in time of need.

Mudfish   Also called *gurnard*, another animal left by ancestors, considered *tapu* and not good to eat.

Pigeons   Maui, the legendary trickster, dressed up like a pigeon to follow his mother without her noticing.

Punga   A goddess who rules everything ugly, and sister to Tane and Tangeroa.

Rangiora   A plant associated with life and prosperity.

Rata   A plant whose red, fluffy flowers are said to take their color from the blood of the hero Tawhaki who fell from the sky.

Raupo   A bulrush whose sweet pollen is used to make cakes resembling gingerbread.

Rengarenga   A New Zealand lily used for food.

Shining Cuckoo   In the spring, this bird's cry means there is not enough food, but in the summer its cry promises success and prosperity.

Spiny Shrub   A plant with poisonous spines left by the jealous ancestor Kupe to punish the Maori.

Sun Orchid   A beautiful flower used for food and decoration.

Tane   God of the earth; of all that walk or crawl or fly.

Tangeroa   God of the sea; of all that swim.

Tapu   Sacred or protected things. *Tapu* things can be dangerous, too.